The Adventures of Ecomunk

The Adventures of Ecomunk

Mr. Beaver Builds a Dam

D. Morgans Bell

VANTAGE PRESS
New York

Illustrated by Janet Kucharnik

Published by Vantage Press, Inc.
516 West 34th Street, New York, New York 10001

Manufactured in the United States of America
ISBN: 0-533-10212-X

Library of Congress Catalog Card No.: 92-90680

0 9 8 7 6 5 4 3 2 1

To my daughter Rebecca, who, to my delight, enjoys
the natural world just as much as I do

Contents

1. Strange Noises at Breakfast   1
2. Mr. Beaver's Plans   6
3. Mrs. Rabbit Seeks Help   11
4. The Message Reaches Ecomunk   18
5. Ecomunk Meets Mrs. Rabbit   25
6. Ecomunk Meets the Beaver   30
7. The Community Has a Meeting   39
8. The Dam Gets Built   44

Appendix: Technical Notes for Young Ecologists   49

The Adventures of Ecomunk

Chapter 1
Strange Noises at Breakfast

Mother Rabbit led her three babies out to the edge of the forest to eat breakfast. The Rabbit family liked to eat the clover leaves that grew at the edge of the woods, near the field of grass that stretched as far as the rabbits could see. The little family of rabbits was peacefully munching away at the tender clover when they heard a loud crash. Now, as you may already know, rabbits are very sensitive to noises; their big ears are well suited for hearing the faintest of sounds. So you can imagine that a loud noise would be rather disturbing to these alert animals. However, after the loud crash, there was silence, and the rabbits went back to their quiet breakfast feeding.

Then the forest and field rang with another loud crash. The rabbits were startled once again, and this time they were so upset that they could not finish their meal. Mother Rabbit decided that she really should find out just what this disturbance was. But first she led her three babies back to the safety of their burrow, and made sure that they understood they were not to budge until she returned. Then she set out for the lower end of the grassy field, from where the loud noises had come.

The field in which the rabbits had been feeding was

at the far end of an old, abandoned farm. Although it seemed like a huge area to the rabbits, to you and me it would be just a small patch of fields that had once been planted in corn. When the farm was abandoned, the wild plants gradually grew back over the fields where corn had grown, and fast-growing trees like cottonwoods, poplars, and birches had already begun to spread their limbs above the wild grasses and shrubs.

Although the abandoned field and the woodlot next to it might not have been much to look at—just an ordinary little area gone wild—it served as home for a wide variety of plants and animals. It had its own little ridges and valleys, rock walls, meadows, and tall trees. It even had a source of clean, running water; a small stream bubbled through a winding channel at the lower corner of the field.

It was toward this stream that Mother Rabbit slowly hopped. The loud, crashing noises had come from this corner, and Mother Rabbit hoped that she could find there the reason for the disturbances in her quiet world. As she made her way down the slope, she saw a flash of movement in an old cherry tree. She immediately froze in her tracks and peered from the corner of her eye to see who or what was moving. She let out a little sigh of relief when she saw it was only a catbird.

Catbirds are gray, medium-size birds that hang about at the fringes of woodlands and feed on a variety of insects. They get their name "catbird" from the variety of catlike noises they can make. The one Mrs. Rabbit had seen was hopping from tree to tree, following her progress through the woods. She turned and said to the bird, "Well, why are you following me? I have

2

business to take care of and don't have time for a bird's foolishness right now."

The catbird replied, "Oh, I'm not fooling around. I heard some loud noises just awhile ago, saw you hopping along, and thought that you might be as curious as I am about the noise."

Mrs. Rabbit said, "I certainly am curious, and I intend to find out what's going on. That noise has disturbed the family breakfast, and I must find out why someone or something is making such a commotion. If you like, come along with me; if you don't want to come, stay here and I'll tell you what I find out on my way back."

The catbird said, "I would appreciate your checking on things. I too am curious, but I'm a little too shy to go zipping down there to check things out."

Mrs. Rabbit said, "Just wait here and let me get on with my business without interruption. When I come back, you'll be the first to know what I've found." With that she spun around and continued hopping down the hill toward the corner of the property.

She paused near the top of the bank leading down to the stream. When she stopped, bent her ears low along her back, and crouched down in the grass, she was nearly invisible and could look and listen before slowly moving closer to the stream.

Finally, she was able to peek over the bank's edge. A flash of movement—something brown—caught her eye. She looked closer and saw a brownish, stocky animal crouched next to a small birch tree near the stream bank. It was a beaver, and it was chewing away at the base of the birch tree, scattering large chunks of bark and woody trunk as it worked.

Mother Rabbit decided to watch the beaver for a

while longer before she made her presence known. She already knew what a beaver was; her parents had described such an animal to her when she was young. However, she had never seen one at work before. The beaver was moving around the tree trunk, taking great bites from the tree with his large, chisel-like front teeth. He had whittled down the tree trunk to where it looked like two pencil points touching at the tips. As Mother Rabbit crouched and watched, the birch tree began to sway back and forth. Slowly at first, then with a rapid swish, the tree toppled over and slammed into the ground. That was the sound the rabbits had heard. It was the beaver, busily at work chopping down trees.

Chapter 2
Mr. Beaver's Plans

Well, it was clear to Mrs. Rabbit that the beaver was not at all concerned about disturbing the animals of the woods and fields. After watching the beaver inspect the tree he had just chopped down and take a first nibble at another sapling, she decided that direct action was called for. She pushed her way through the fringe of shrubs behind which she had been hiding and hopped down the bank toward the busy beaver.

The beaver must have seen her out of the corner of his eye, for he immediately ran to the stream and leaped into the water, giving a loud slap of his tail when he ducked under the surface. After a few moments, he poked his snout out of the water and looked around warily. Mother Rabbit said, "There is no need for alarm. I only want to ask you a few questions."

The beaver studied her carefully for a minute, then climbed up onto the stream bank, sat back on his hind legs, and said, "Okay. Now that you have disrupted my work, please tell me what it is you want."

Mother Rabbit said, "Mr. Beaver, we rabbits are not used to hearing such loud noises in the meadow where we feed. Must you really make so much noise? And just what on earth do you plan to do with all of these trees you have chopped down?"

Mr. Beaver replied, "Well, ma'am, as you have noted, I am a beaver. We beavers do one thing better than any other animal—we build dams. My plan is to build a dam right here. I will cut down a lot of these small trees and pile them together to block the flow of water in the stream. After I get that done, I can use mud from the stream bank to patch the holes between the tree trunks. Gradually, the waters of the stream will back up and form a pool at the lower end of the meadow. In that pool, I will build a house of large branches—we beavers call it a lodge—and raise my family there. This is what my father did, as did my father's father, and many generations of beavers before me."

Mother Rabbit looked at him doubtfully. She said, "I understand that you have this natural urge to build dams, and looking at those big front teeth of yours, I can see that you are able to cut down trees quite easily. But do you have to do all of this right here in our meadow? Can't you do this dam building somewhere else?"

Mr. Beaver took a brief moment before answering. "Mother Rabbit," he said, "I realize that you may consider this an inconvenience, but what other choice do I have? I came from over that mountain to the east; my brother and his family have their dam across a stream in the next valley. I checked the land south of this meadow, but the humans have built their homes right next to the water down there. They will probably tear down anything that I build, and their dogs and cats will chase me and try to harm my family—once I manage to get a family started."

Although Mother Rabbit realized that the beaver had honest intentions, she still replied sharply, "An

inconvenience, is that what it will be? I fully understand the problems of raising a family these days.
Father Rabbit and myself had to do quite a bit of
searching before we found this spot. We too came
upstream, away from the humans, to find a quieter,
safer place to live and raise our family."

Then she repeated, "An inconvenience, is that what
it would be? Tell me, Mr. Beaver, just how big will the
dam be? And what will it do to the meadow and the
woodlands? Will we still have a place to live and feed
when you are finished, or will we be forced to move by
the rising waters?"

Mr. Beaver answered, "Well, I guess that the dam
will be about as big as I want it to be. Obviously, some
of this meadow and woodlands will be flooded, but I
cannot tell you just how much. So I can't really tell you
whether your home or feeding areas will be flooded or
will remain dry."

Mother Rabbit, on hearing these vague plans, was
even more upset and said as much to the beaver. "This
is distressing news," she said. "I understand your
desire to build here, but it sounds like you are just
going to let the chips fall where they may." (Mother
Rabbit, ordinarily a quiet, ladylike animal, did have a
subtle sense of humor and an ear for the pun.) She
added, "I think that this is going to change things
around here, but I don't think that the changes are all
going to be good."

With these words, she turned on her heels and
hopped up the bank. As she slowly made her way back
to the burrow, part of her mind continued to think
about the arrival of the beaver and the effects that his
dam-building activities could have on her and on the
peaceful world in which she lived. She and her family

had become used to the cycle of seasons—the normal sequence of changes that made each year seem such a complete unit. She recalled the growth and rich promise of spring, the endless warm days and nights of summer, the scarlet splendor and crisp mornings of autumn, and the snow-covered vistas of winter. But this new change taking place down at the meadow's edge was something that had taken her by surprise and, perhaps, needed some discussion by the other animals residing on the old farmland.

Chapter 3
Mrs. Rabbit Seeks Help

A short distance from her burrow, Mrs. Rabbit saw the catbird perched on the limb of a cottonwood tree. "Well now," said the bird, "just what did you find out down there? Is there something going on that I should know about?"

Mrs. Rabbit replied, "There is a beaver cutting down trees in the lower corner of the meadow. He says that he intends to build a dam there, flood part of the meadow, and begin to raise a family."

"How's that?" said the catbird. "He is going to flood the meadow? What about all of the meadow animals—their families, their homes, their food supplies?"

Mrs. Rabbit said, "Catbird, that is precisely what worries me. That beaver is going to do his thing down there by the creek and the rest of us will just have to suffer. I don't know what we can do to change that."

The catbird replied, "I know a lot of the animals, especially the birds, in this part of the woods. Let me make a few calls (the catbird had a sense of humor that matched Mrs. Rabbit's) and I'll see what advice I can get. There must be someone out there who can help us protect our families."

Actually, the catbird had a pretty good idea of where he was going to go to look for help. You see, some species of birds often group together for their spring and fall migrations, and when they are in these large flocks, they talk together a great deal. You may have heard the chattering of starlings or cowbirds as they gathered by the thousands in trees; you can imagine the amount of talking that is going on at these times. After spending a day or so in one of these large flocks, every bird in the flock is up to date on the latest gossip.

The catbird had been hanging around the edges of one of these flocks the previous fall and had heard some of the birds talking about a similar situation that had taken place. Who was it that had helped out? Oh yes, it had been one of those bossy chipmunks. That had struck the catbird as a bit strange; who would think that a chipmunk could have much to do with how the other animals acted. But that was what the birds had been talking about, and it was worth checking into.

Now, how to do it? The catbird figured that the smart thing to do would be to ask a local chipmunk. After all, if the birds' gossip was true, then maybe the chipmunk gossip had more details, and he could get some advice on whom to talk with.

With this thought, the catbird spread his wings and flew off through the trees. He headed for an old rock wall that ran along the edge of the abandoned farm property. He knew that the old wall provided a wonderful habitat for chipmunks, who lived in the holes and crannies that were found among the rocks.

The catbird flew down to the wall and alit on a large rock. Within a few minutes, he saw a furry little head poke out from among the stones. It was one of the local chipmunks. The catbird said, "Hello there. May I talk with you for a minute?"

The chipmunk stared at him with sharp brown

eyes, finally deciding that things were safe enough to venture out of the hole. "What is it you want?" he said in his clear, high-pitched voice.

The catbird said, "I recall hearing last year about a problem that was solved by a chipmunk. Would you know anything about that?"

The chipmunk said, "We chipmunks have solved a lot of problems in the past year. To which particular problem are you referring?"

The catbird, caught a little off guard by the quick response of the chipmunk, said, "Well, I don't know all of the details. I just know that some of the animals were having a problem, and that the problem was settled by a chipmunk."

The chipmunk thought this over for a short time and then said, "Well, the best thing for me to do is to refer you to Ecomunk. He'll know what to do next."

"Ecomunk?" exclaimed the catbird. "Just who, or what, is an Ecomunk?"

The chipmunk said, "You mean that you have never heard of Ecomunk? I thought everyone had heard of him. Why, half of the problems of the animals in these woods get referred to him. And you have no idea who he is?"

"Well," stammered the catbird, "I knew that you chipmunks were involved in helping other animals with their ecological problems. But is Ecomunk one of you? Is he, or she, a chipmunk? Or is Ecomunk some kind of weird creature that someone developed?"

"No, no," the chipmunk said reassuringly, "Ecomunk is actually a shortened name for the Ecological Society of Chipmunks—a society of chipmunks that specializes in helping other animals. But generally only one chipmunk is sent to solve a particular problem, so we refer to him or her as the Ecomunk."

"Now it is beginning to make a little bit of sense," said the catbird. "There is a society of chipmunks that helps animals with their environmental problems—am I correct?"

"Precisely so," said the chipmunk.

"And you," continued the catbird, "often call the representative of this society the Ecomunk—right?"

"Correct again," said the chipmunk, swishing his bushy tail with impatience. "That's it in a nutshell!"

"Well, this Ecomunk must be some sort of super-animal," said the catbird. "I just don't see how a chipmunk, who must weigh all of one half of a pound, can step into a situation with rabbits and beavers and other large animals and solve their problems."

"I can assure you that size is not the most impor-tant factor in these matters," said the chipmunk. "We chipmunks don't rely on pushing others around to solve problems. It doesn't make any sense to try that. The secret to the success of any effective Ecomunk is that the Ecomunk sent to the job has a good under-standing of the environment—how natural systems work and how various animals fit into natural systems. And further, the Ecomunk has no reason for favoring one group of animals over another group."

"Except maybe yourselves," snapped the catbird. "If you chipmunks are so good at coming up with all of the answers, then you could really make all the decisions favor the chipmunks."

"The Ecological Society of Chipmunks has strict rules of conduct to prevent any such misbehavior," answered the chipmunk, a little upset that the catbird would even hint at such actions. "Although, I might

add, most animals don't seem to share your concern; after all, look at the lives that chipmunks lead. Do you see chipmunks driving other animals out of house and home, using up all of the food or nesting places? No, you don't see such behavior, and there is a good reason that you don't—we chipmunks have an economical way of living. We eat small amounts of all kinds of seeds, nuts, and berries; we use all kinds of nooks, crannies, and holes for our homes; and we rarely bother other animals."

He continued, "Why, you can walk through a path of woods and never know there are dozens of chipmunks living there; they are always around, but their lives are so quiet that their presence is rarely noticed. Believe me, we chipmunks practice what we preach— we do try to live quietly and peacefully in our environments."

This was a rather long speech for a chipmunk, but this particular one was a little upset that the catbird had even thought that the chipmunks might misuse their environmental knowledge.

"That all sounds just peachy," said the catbird, somewhat sarcastically. "I'm looking forward to seeing just how you chipmunks operate. And before we forget why I'm here, we have the business with Mrs. Rabbit to take care of. She is concerned about the effects of a dam that a beaver is building at the corner of Sloane's old farm." (Mr. Sloane, by the way, was the farmer who had worked the land at one time, before he moved to be nearer to his children and grandchildren.) "Mrs. Rabbit and I agree that some outside help is needed to make sure that the beaver's dam-building activity doesn't cause harm to other animals."

"That is certainly a problem for Ecomunk," said the

chipmunk. "I will do this. I will arrange to have an Ecomunk come out here as soon as possible. In the meantime, you fly back and tell Mrs. Rabbit and the other animals of Sloane's farm to sit tight and wait for help to arrive."

Chapter 4
The Message Reaches Ecomunk

Actually, the chipmunk had no real reason to be mysterious about his plans for reaching Ecomunk—he was just acting that way in front of the catbird to make himself sound a little more important. In fact, the Ecomunk network had a well-developed, very efficient method of reaching out to all the animals.

The many chipmunks living in forests, fields, and even near people's homes acted as scouts to recognize and report local environmental problems. The messengers for Ecomunk were often crows; these birds lived in all parts of the country and could rapidly carry messages from the chipmunk scouts to Ecomunk. In addition, the crows, being naturally curious and intelligent, could keep their sharp eyes on what was happening in the fields and forests below at all times.

The chipmunk scurried down the tunnel of his burrow to a little, round-sided chamber, not the large one that stored his seed and nuts, but a smaller one that held several pieces of aluminum foil. He selected five pieces of foil and hurried back to the entrance of his burrow. On a nearby clear area, he arranged the five pieces of foil in the pattern of a cross—one piece in the center of the pattern and the four pieces on the four sides of the center piece. The pieces of shiny foil could be easily seen by a crow flying above, while the pattern of the pieces let the crow know there was a message to be delivered to Ecomunk.

After setting up this visual signal, the chipmunk quickly scurried back to the safety of his burrow, where he settled into his feeding chamber and nibbled on a cheekful of dried seeds taken from his storeroom.

After a wait of about twenty minutes, the chipmunk heard the fluttering of strong wings outside his burrow. He ran to the entrance and peeked out just in time to see the dark shape of a crow landing at the clearing where the chipmunk had placed his shiny signal. He was relieved to see that it was Corvus, a crow who roosted in a great oak tree in the forest. He had worked with Corvus before and was pleased to see a familiar face.

"Well, my furry little friend," cawed Corvus, "what is the fuss about this time? It seems we never talk except when there is trouble afoot."

The chipmunk replied, "I think that we have another job for Ecomunk. Mrs. Rabbit, from over by the old fields, has said that a beaver is at work constructing a dam. She and the other animals who live there are afraid their homes are in danger, and they have requested the help of Ecomunk."

Corvus cocked his head and said, "Well, that is what Ecomunk does best—solve problems like this. I will fly right away to his burrow and tell him that his help is needed. I presume, by the way, that the dam is not yet finished and there is time to settle this matter before the waters start to rise?"

The chipmunk replied, "I think the beaver has just begun his work. Mrs. Rabbit found out about it because she heard the sound of falling trees."

19

"In that case, we have time to solve this problem before any lasting damage is done," said Corvus. "That is a pleasant change; too many times we find out about these things when it is too late to save all the homes of the animals. Sit tight here; I'm off to tell Ecomunk of the problem."

With this farewell, the crow hopped several times, flapped his heavy wings, and flew off into the trees. The chipmunk retired once again to the safety of his warm burrow, content for the moment with the knowledge that he had done his part to bring help to Mrs. Rabbit and her friends.

The crow flapped steadily in the direction of a high mountain ridge to the west. The local Ecomunk's head-quarters was just under the crest of that ridge, about four miles away (as the crow flies, of course). In several minutes of hard flying, the crow could spot the flat slab of rock that stretched out in front of Ecomunk's bur-row. He angled down toward this and alit with all the grace a crow can muster during a difficult landing on a windswept ledge.

Ecomunk's burrow was not your average chip-munk habitat. Because of his work, he had to be prepared to receive a wide variety of visitors, who could come in all sizes and shapes. (Although the crows brought many of the messages from chipmunk scouts, some larger animals made the hike up the ridge them-selves to request Ecomunk's help.) But though he was an unusual animal, he was still a chipmunk, and he still liked to live in the style that chipmunks had enjoyed for centuries. So there was a large flat area just under the top of the ridge where his animal guests could arrive, a wide space under an overhanging rock where he could sit to converse with his guests, and a

series of tunnels, weaving back under and between the rocks, that looked just like any other chipmunk's burrow.

At the time the crow was landing on the ledge outside his burrow, Ecomunk was relaxing in his living chamber, reading over a newsletter that outlined new human rules for the protection of wetlands. (Yes, Ecomunks are able to read what humans write; there is a story about this that will be told in another adventure.) Ecomunk was well aware that wetlands areas had been filled in, dried up, altered, rearranged, and in many other ways abused. The Ecological Society of Chipmunks had made a valiant effort to protect the organisms living in wetlands, but there is a limit to the things chipmunks can accomplish in front of oncoming bulldozers. But he was glad to see that the humans were finally coming around to understanding that stricter protection was needed. Ecomunk tried to stay informed on the rules that humans enacted to protect the environment, realizing full well that he could give them some rich advice on how to go about such protection if he only had the opportunity.

When he heard the flapping of wings outside his burrow, Ecomunk folded the newsletter and hurried to the open space near the overhang. Corvus was standing there, making little adjustments in his flight feathers with his glossy black bill. "Hello there, Ecomunk," said Corvus. "I bring a message concerning a Mrs. Rabbit, who lives down on Sloane's old farm."

"Aha," said Ecomunk, "I'll bet my winter acorns she has an environmental problem that needs our attention."

"You are, as usual, right on the mark," said Corvus. "Mrs. Rabbit and the other animals in that community are worried that a beaver will flood out their homes with water from a dam he is building. She has talked with the beaver, but he appears to be dead set on building his dam exactly when and where he wants to. They need some help from you, Ecomunk!"

"That's what I'm here for," exclaimed Ecomunk. "If you will be so kind as to wait here for a few minutes, I'll pack my field gear and put on my flying harness. Then you can drop me off at the burrow of the chipmunk scout. I'll start by having him fill me in on the local conditions."

Ecomunk ducked back into his burrow and grabbed a field pack that he kept at the ready for just such occasions. He then took down a strange-looking leather harness that could fit across his back, extend under his arms, and buckle tight across his chest and waist. The harness had a strong loop that stood out from his back; the crow was able to grasp this loop in his strong claws and hoist the chipmunk into the air. With the help of this flying rig and the wings of the friendly crow, Ecomunk could travel distances that would take him days to cover on his own little legs (although Ecomunk was an important animal in the community, he was not much bigger than any other chipmunk that you might see in your yard). With this gear in hand, he hurried back out to where the crow was patiently waiting.

Corvus had been through all this preparation before; he waited patiently while Ecomunk slipped into his flying harness and buckled it securely. Then the crow hopped forward and wrapped the claws of one foot around the loop on the harness. With a grunt, he heaved himself and Ecomunk off the rock ledge and into the air. As he took the first few strong flaps that

23

would keep them airborne, he reached down and took hold of the loop on the harness with his other foot. Thus secured, the pair winged out over the valley and headed back to the burrow of the chipmunk scout.

Chapter 5

Ecomunk Meets Mrs. Rabbit

The flight back to the chipmunk's burrow took only a short time, but Ecomunk enjoyed every minute of it. Every time he took a trip like this with the help of the crow, he marvelled at the beautiful view his lofty seat gave him.

From his vantage point, dangling from the strong claws of the crow, Ecomunk had a view that few chipmunks were ever privileged to see. He could see the patchwork of woods and old fields below, with dirt roads bounding the fields and silvery streams trickling through the woods. To the left, a small lake glinted like a silver coin set in the green of the woods. It was late in the spring, and the trees and grasses had developed rich, green leaves turned up to catch the life-giving sunlight.

The view was spectacular, and Ecomunk tried, as he did every time, to memorize the entire picture in front of him. In this way, he could sit back, close his eyes, and see the wonderful view again in his mind when he was back in the closeness of his burrow.

Too soon, the marvelous trip was over, and the crow was dipping down through the canopy of green leaves marking the woods where the scout chipmunk lived. Corvus dropped down near the ground and, with a rapid flapping of his wings, hovered just above a thick patch of moss. He released his grip on the leather harness that held Ecomunk, allowing the chipmunk to tumble gracefully to the earth, well cushioned by the lush mosses. The crow then flapped up to a perch on a limb of a nearby white oak tree and busied himself rearranging his flight feathers.

Ecomunk wriggled out of his leather flying harness, grabbed his field bag, and scampered over to the chipmunk's burrow. That chipmunk, alerted to their arrival by the flapping of the crow's wings, was already waiting at the mouth of his burrow. "Welcome, Ecomunk," said the chipmunk. "You didn't waste any time in getting here."

"No," said Ecomunk, "you caught me at a convenient moment. I'd just gotten back from settling a dispute between some squirrels and a pileated woodpecker. The woodpecker was raising such a racket that the squirrels were going nutty, if you'll excuse the expression. But that's a story for later. For now, we have a new problem to solve. At least, that is what the crow told me."

The scout chipmunk replied, "Yes, this one may take more than a little effort on your part. Mrs. Rabbit and her neighbors are quite upset about a dam that a beaver is building down in the corner of Mr. Sloane's old farm. This beaver just showed up one day, started chopping down trees, and is well along on the construction of the base of a new dam. What's more, he doesn't seem to care what the other animals think about his actions or what his dam might do to affect the other animals living in that area."

"Well, the beaver may not realize that he can't just make changes in the environment without first dis-

cussing it with the other animals, especially those that might be affected by his construction," said Ecomunk. "After all, he is probably new in this area, and this may be his first dam. Perhaps he was living at a dam that his parents built and was not told how to go about preparing to build his own home. In any case, we can go to speak with him and discuss these things. But on our way, we will first stop and let Mrs. Rabbit know that we are on the job."

"Are we all going down to face the beaver?" asked the scout, with more than a little eagerness. He was anxious to participate in the details of the job because he had dreams of becoming an Ecomunk some day in the future. And what better way to get experience than to work with the local Ecomunk in the field!

Ecomunk replied, "It is all right for you to come down there with me, as long as you let me do most of the talking. Your assistance is important because you are familiar with the local animals and their feelings about this thing.

"But," he added, "I don't want to take Mrs. Rabbit or any of her friends along on this first visit; I want to meet the beaver and speak with him before he has to talk in front of an angry crowd. He may be surprised to find out that he cannot alter the environment without first checking with the local community, and I want him to give that idea some thought before he meets with the others."

With those words of caution, Ecomunk hoisted up his field pack, turned to the chipmunk scout, and said, "Which way to Mrs. Rabbit's burrow? Let's get this show on the road."

The scout instantly became serious and replied,

"We just walk toward the east for about a quarter of a mile. Her burrow is at the base of a little grassy knoll."

The two chipmunks turned toward the noonday sun (which is slightly toward the south in the spring), turned once again to their left, and set out briskly toward the east. The day was pleasantly warm, and they fully enjoyed their brisk hike through the woods. Ecomunk had never been on this abandoned farm property before, but he cheerfully greeted the resident animals that watched his progress through their neighborhood.

After about half an hour of brisk hiking, the pair saw a grassy knoll ahead. That was where the rabbits' burrow was located. The chipmunks did not want to frighten Mrs. Rabbit or her children, so they called out loudly, "Hello, hello! We are here to talk with Mrs. Rabbit. Please come out and see us."

Within a minute, they saw the sleek head and long ears of Mrs. Rabbit appear in the mouth of the burrow. Seeing the chipmunks standing there, she quickly hopped forward to greet them.

Chapter 6
Ecomunk Meets the Beaver

Mrs. Rabbit had become so anxious while waiting for the appearance of Ecomunk that she almost forgot her manners in her haste to talk. But she quickly recovered her composure and said with utmost politeness, "Good afternoon, sirs. I am Mrs. Martha Rabbit, and I want to thank you for taking the time to visit our humble habitat. Have you been informed of our problem?"

Ecomunk, being equally polite, responded, "Good afternoon, ma'am. I am the resident Ecomunk and this is my assistant on this case. We are only too glad to come to help the animals in this community. And, yes, I have a basic understanding of the situation. Has anything new happened since you talked with my assistant here?"

"No," said Mrs Rabbit. "The situation is basically the same as before. I am not very good at debating issues like these, so I decided that I would leave the matter in your capable hands."

"That is probably best," said Ecomunk. "I can modestly admit that I have had a lot of experience in such matters. Now, I understand that you would like me to speak firmly with the beaver about the environmental effects of his dam building. Is there anything else that I should know before we leave?"

Seeing Mrs. Rabbit shake her head no, Ecomunk hitched up his field pack, winked at the scout chipmunk, and said, "All right, sit tight, and let us make your fight." (He always did his best to lighten up serious situations like these.) "We should be back before sundown." With these parting words, he spun on his heels and set out briskly for the lower corner of the old, abandoned field, followed closely by the anxious scout chipmunk.

The walk was pleasant for the pair of chipmunks, and they chatted with each other about the rich diversity of plant and animal life that flourished in the small habitat. They didn't talk about the upcoming job but rather enjoyed the sights, sounds, and smells of the woods and fields.

They had not yet reached the stream on which the beaver was building his dam when they heard the swish of a falling tree, followed by the thud of the trunk hitting the ground. Ecomunk said, "I don't blame Mrs. Rabbit for being upset—even the noise of dam building is disturbing. I hope that the beaver is not too far along on his construction; it is easier to discuss environmental impacts with a builder before he or she gets a project half-completed."

Ecomunk and his companion came over the bank where Mrs. Rabbit had paused to watch the beaver and moved slowly down toward the stream. To their right, they could see the dark, bulky form of the beaver as he moved through the cluster of birches, seeking another tree of a size suitable for his dam. "Hello there," said Ecomunk. "Could you spare a minute to talk some business with us?"

The beaver walked heavily over to them, paused to take a few long, slow breaths, and said, "I do need a

31

little break; this dam building is tiring work. But what business could I possibly have with a pair of chipmunks?"

"Allow me to introduce myself," said Ecomunk. "I am the resident Ecomunk for the area, and I am responding to concerns voiced by the community about your building project. If you have not heard of the Ecological Society of Chipmunks, I can tell you briefly that we are responsible for monitoring the overall health of both the local environment and the plants and animals that live in it. Almost all of the animal species recognize our role and cooperate with us to produce greater environmental harmony."

"Bully for you," said the beaver, somewhat rudely. "But just what does that have to do with me? All that I am doing is building a dam—I need the pond for protection and for a place to build my lodge. We beavers have always done this without having other animals hassle us. I don't remember any chipmunks bothering my dad when he was working on his dam."

"Well, these are changing times," said Ecomunk. "Nowadays, the things that animals do are looked at very closely. We in the animal community are not set against your building a dam—we just want to see what effect it might have on the environment. Perhaps we can make suggestions about how you can build without having to harm any of the animals. I assure you that, in the end, your cooperation will mean a better environment and more harmony among the animals in this community. Now, if you don't mind, why don't you show me what you intend to do here?"

The beaver had been standing there scowling at this little lecture that the Ecomunk had been delivering. But at this last request, the beaver's attitude

brightened visibly. Being a master builder, he was always proud to demonstrate his planning and engineering skills. He turned toward the stream and, pointing, said, "See where the stream gets narrow down between those sloping banks? That is where I can place a dam and cause the water to back up into the meadow."

The beaver continued, "That spot is very favorable for blocking the stream, and the pond I will create with the dam will reach that grove of aspens over there. That means that I will be able to reach those trees without getting too far from the water. Beavers use the aspens for food—we eat the bark—and use the bare poles for building and repairing our dams and beaver lodges. Down there, where the stream runs more slowly, I saw some mud banks. That is where I can get the mud I use for patching holes among the trees that I pile together to form the center of the dam."

"A fine piece of engineering," said Ecomunk, in a way meant to make the beaver feel more comfortable with his next set of questions. "Could you tell me how high the water will come and how much of the meadow will be flooded?"

"That is easy enough," said the beaver, happy to talk more about his plans. "I will make the top of the dam a little lower than the tops of those sloping banks. In that way, the stream banks will contain the water and the overflow will pass over my dam. I don't want the water to flow over the sloping banks, because that will erode the soil and eventually drain my pond. Now, if I make the dam just a bit lower than the banks, then the dam will cause the water to reach a level equal to the height of the dam. If you take a straight stick, hold it level, and look along it (and here he picked up a stick to demonstrate his point), you can see where the edge of the water will come. It will reach as far as that large oak on the left, as far as that old cherry tree in the center, and as far as the grove of aspens on the right."

"Elegantly done," murmured Ecomunk. "I am impressed with your skills in planning this project. You seem to have a firm grasp of the engineering needed for dam building. But when a builder begins construction work in a community of plants and animals, he needs to consider additional facts—how the other animals and plants live their lives and how they will be affected by the change. That information has to be used in the design of the dam, just as you talked about using information on the flow of the stream. That's the way we plan projects in this era of environmental concern."

That was another rather long speech for Ecomunk, but he felt that it was necessary to let the beaver know how things were going to go in the future. The beaver, having never heard such a presentation before, was a little upset. "Does that mean I can't build a dam the way I want to build it?" he said, anger showing in his voice. "What gives you the right to come over here and tell me what to do?"

"Those are two different questions," said Ecomunk calmly; he was not about to get drawn into the beaver's angry talk. "First, we are not telling you that you can't build a dam—in fact, a dam in this meadow might be a very scenic and valuable addition to the habitat here. But before it is constructed, all of the animals who live here have the right to hear your plan and comment on how they feel about it."

Ecomunk continued his calm response to the beaver's angry questions. "In answer to your second question, we get our right to review your project by agreement with all of the animals living here. They recognize the importance of these environmental reviews and have given us the authority to act as we do. Our goal is to keep balance in the biological community, and we work very hard to approach that goal. Of course, there is no written law that we enforce, but the rest of the animals trust our judgment. We can't punish you for ignoring our advice, but if you act against the wishes of this community, you will not have many friends here."

"That sounds like a threat," said the beaver. He was still defensive about having his plans reviewed by these strangers. "You know that there are not many animals who can push me around."

"I don't doubt that," said Ecomunk, taking careful note of the strong muscles of the beaver. "We have no intention of pushing. Rather, we hope to guide you in certain directions in your planning. We may be able to give you some advice on how big your dam should be or how you might fill it with water without harming the animals in the meadow."

"Call it what you may," blustered the beaver, "advice, guidance, or review—it still sounds like interference to me. But let us see how this might work. You have said that you can 'advise' me on how big my dam might be. Well, I plan to have four feet of water around my home—my beaver lodge. How does that sit with your environmental planning?"

Ecomunk thought that over for a few moments, and then said, "If that is so, then the water in the dam will extend as far as that cherry tree. Is that correct? And that little mound of dirt you see in front of that tree marks a groundhog hole, I believe." He turned to the chipmunk scout and said, "Am I correct? Is that a groundhog's hole?"

The chipmunk scout, delighted to make a contribution to the discussion, said, "Yes, a groundhog lives right there. He is an elderly chap whom we call Harvey. He has lived there for nearly four years. He knows everyone in the meadow and woods, and he is one of the nicest groundhogs that you could have the pleasure of meeting."

"Is that so?" said Ecomunk. "I am willing to bet that Harvey won't look forward to having water pouring down into his burrow. We could check with him on that, but I'm pretty sure that he would have a problem with it."

"So what!" said the beaver. "He can move and dig a new burrow. After all, that is what groundhogs do best."

"But why should he have to go to such trouble if it is not necessary?" replied Ecomunk. "Let's look at this problem from a different angle. Tell me, where have you planned to build your lodge?"

"Right next to that old stump over there," said the beaver, pointing with a stout paw. "That spot really caught my eye."

"Well," said Ecomunk, "if you moved the location of your lodge about twenty feet to the east, you would not need to fill the dam so high to get four feet of water around your lodge. Is that not correct?"

"Yes, that is correct," said the beaver, after taking a careful look at these areas of the dam site.

"Then you could have a lodge with the right amount of water around it and still spare old Harvey's burrow, couldn't you?" said Ecomunk, driving his point home.

"Yes, I guess I could at that," said the beaver. "That

new spot is just as good for my lodge, Harvey wouldn't have to learn to swim, and I wouldn't have to build my dam so high. Come to think of it, I would save time and energy too." He scratched his nose rather sheepishly and said, "You know, this planning may not be as bad as I thought."

"It isn't bad at all," replied Ecomunk. "In fact, environmental planning is just as interesting as engineering a structure such as a dam. And the results wind up being of more benefit to more animals in the long run. Now that you have seen what we consider in these matters, perhaps you can make some additional changes before meeting with all of the animals tonight."

"What meeting are you talking about?" asked the beaver. "Do I have to sit and be criticized by every animal in the area? I really don't see why I have to be put to all this trouble over a silly little dam."

"But this is the most important part of building, at least as far as the other animals are concerned," said Ecomunk. "These open meetings allow all of the animals to hear what you are doing to their environment, and I mean that seriously—*their environment!* We will expect to see you at seven in the evening, in the clearing by the large stumps. Any of the woodland animals can give you directions to that place."

Chapter 7
The Community Has a Meeting

The community meeting took place that evening as planned. Mrs. Rabbit and Ecomunk's chipmunk helper had hurried busily through the forest and fields, notifying all the animals that there were important issues to be discussed. The clearing by the large stumps soon began to fill with small animals—squirrels, rabbits, groundhogs, opossums, muskrats, mice, voles (a kind of short-tailed mouse), raccoons, chipmunks, and even flying squirrels. There were also many species of birds—sparrows, wrens, flycatchers, chickadees, warblers, cardinals, jays, crows, and many others. They all were gathered to make their voices heard about the beaver's dam project.

You may note that I have not mentioned anything about larger mammals like foxes, bears, or wolves; or about birds like hawks, eagles, or owls. Well, the reason is obvious—although Ecomunk was respected for his judgment and advice on ecological matters, he was not dominant in stature or voice, and he could not guarantee the safety of the smaller organisms if these predators were at the meeting. So they were not invited. But in a way, the interests of these larger animals were indirectly represented at the meeting; the predators depended from day to day on the continued success of the smaller animals and it was in their own best

39

interests to have the smaller animals flourish around the dam.

The animals chattered excitedly in small groups, some passing on news that they. had heard, others learning about the project for the first time. The noise died away quickly when Ecomunk, his chipmunk helper, Mr. Beaver, and Mrs. Rabbit came forward to face the group.

Ecomunk was the first to speak. "This meeting will come to order," he said with firm authority. "We are here to hear and comment on the plans that Mr. Beaver has for a dam. After he speaks (without interruption, please!), the floor will be open to questions. At that time, feel free to speak openly; this is the time when your opinion will be heard and can affect the project. So don't sit silently now and complain later. Now, Mr. Beaver, you make your presentation."

Mr. Beaver spoke at some length, setting forth the design of his dam in much the same way as he had told Ecomunk earlier in the day. A careful observer could tell that he was a little nervous; he shifted from foot to foot and talked in a somewhat higher tone than he normally used. But he managed to get through his talk, even describing the changes that he had made to spare Harvey (you do remember Harvey the woodchuck, don't you?) the shock of being submerged.

After the beaver had finished with his talk, Ecomunk arose and said, "At this time, any one of you can ask the beaver a question about his project. Please raise your hand and be recognized before speaking."

Mrs. Rabbit, being the first of the animals to become aware of the beaver's activities, was the first to pose a question. She said to Mr. Beaver, "Your project creates an awful lot of noise and disturbs our activities.

How long do you intend to make these loud noises, and is there anything that you can do to work more quiet-ly?"

The beaver answered, "I can't cut down trees without making noise. Actually, most of the tree cutting will be done in about two weeks; after that, I'll only cut down a tree once in a while. I don't see any way around the noise problem."

Ecomunk spoke up quickly, saying, "It's not quite that hopeless, I feel. As I understand it, Mrs. Rabbit and her family were disturbed while eating their morn-ing meal, just about dawn. Is there any way that you could do other, more quiet jobs in the early morning, and then do your tree cutting after most of the animals have had a chance to get their morning meal?"

"Well, the thought of not getting to work cutting trees at the crack of dawn is a little strange to me," said the beaver, "but I suppose I could adjust my hours to give the others a little quiet time in the morning. OK, consider it done; I won't start cutting trees until two hours after sunrise."

"Well done, Mr. Beaver," responded Ecomunk. "That's the type of thinking that makes things easier for us all. Now, are there other questions?"

There were two otters in the audience, and one of these playful creatures rose to speak. "We otters get our food from the creek, and we also use the banks of the creek for play—we make mud slides on the bank. How do we know that we will still be able to use the creek for fishing and playing when your dam is com-pleted?"

The beaver, having a good grasp of the engineering involved in dam building, replied, "Well, the stream will never be dammed completely. My dam will reduce the amount of water flowing in the stream for a while as it fills up, but the change in water flow will be pretty small. Once the dam is completed, the water will continue to flow over the dam and down the creek. I might add that the dam will cut down on the amount of flooding that occurs downstream; it serves as a flood-control measure. And last, you and your relatives are certainly welcome to fish and play in the pond my dam will create. We beavers eat plants and enjoy a bit of play ourselves; your fishing and playing won't bother us at all."

The questioning of the beaver went on for another hour, with the more timid of the animals finally getting the nerve to ask the questions that had been bothering them. In all, it was a useful question-and-answer session, and both the beaver and the other animals became much more familiar with each others' lives and worries.

After the questioning died down, Ecomunk rose and said, "I think that we have covered most of the major problems tonight. Now that you folks are acquainted with Mr. Beaver and can see that his intentions are sincere, you should feel free to talk with him at any time about his dam and how it affects each of you. And I am sure that Mr. Beaver will, in turn, take the time to talk with you when needed. Mr. Beaver, you have our thanks for coming here tonight and answering the questions of the animals of the community."

With this closing speech, the animals rose and moved off to their homes in small groups, still discussing how the dam would make their environment slightly different. They were somewhat reassured by the meeting, and vowed to hold the beaver to the plans that he had promised.

Chapter 8
The Dam Gets Built

With the air cleared about the effects of the dam, Mr. Beaver worked diligently to complete his construction work. As the dam grew higher and stronger, the water from the creek formed a beautiful pool behind the dam. True to his promise, the beaver built the dam so that the home of Harvey the woodchuck was kept high and dry. In fact, Harvey had a home with a new, fabulous view of the pond, and he also found good eating in the lush plant growth that sprouted on the banks of the pond.

Mrs. Rabbit and her family were able to eat breakfast undisturbed by the sound of falling trees, and the rabbits often followed their breakfast with a stroll down to the shores of the pond. Despite the angry way in which Mrs. Rabbit and Mr. Beaver had met, they became rather close friends and enjoyed chatting each day.

The otters who had been concerned about the stream found that the fish downstream remained as plentiful as ever, and they grew even fatter than before because of the abundant food washed downstream from the pond.

The pond filled up slowly as the beaver worked on the dam, and the little animals of the fields—the insects, salamanders, mice, and voles—had plenty of time to move to higher ground in an orderly manner. Once the animals of the old farm community got used to the presence of the dam, it quickly became a focal point in many of their daily activities.

All of these changes, of course, affected the overall ecology of the area. Where old pasture had once been, there was now a pond with open water and beds of water plants. These changes in the habitat caused some small shifts in the numbers and kinds of animals that could live comfortably in the new surroundings. But this is the very nature of natural systems; as those systems change, different types of plants and animals benefit from the changes. On the whole, the beaver's dam probably was a good thing for the communities of plants and animals living at this corner of Mr. Sloane's old farm. Clear, clean water is a very important resource for all living creatures, and where it forms ponds or lakes, animals tend to gather.

Meanwhile, Ecomunk returned to his comfortable burrow high on the cliff and settled down to await another request for help from concerned animals. He felt good about how the beaver had worked things out with the residents of the old farm and hoped that future problems would be solved in as peaceful a manner. For he knew that there would be more problems as different groups of plants and animals grew together in their natural habitats, and he also knew that the wisdom of the Ecological Society of Chipmunks was going to be called upon to solve many of these problems.

His spring had already started out with a busy schedule, and Ecomunk knew that things would only get busier. Many of the animals found shelter during

the winter and slowed their activities to almost nothing. Some even hibernated through the winter. But in springtime, the forests and fields bustled with new activity as animals prepared to raise new families and build new homes or burrows. With all of this renewed activity, he knew that he and other Ecomunks like him would be called upon to give advice in all sorts of situations.

Ecomunk didn't mind the prospect of being busy; every new job or request for help meant that his society would be helping the community of animals run a little more smoothly. But for the meantime, Ecomunk settled for a little relaxation, a large helping of crunchy seeds from his storerooms, and some time to look out over the beautiful forest that he could see from the front of his burrow.

Appendix: Technical Notes for Young Ecologists

Species Profiles

When ecologists decide to study a particular animal or group of plants or animals, they generally begin their studies by gathering available information about the organisms. This is termed a "literature review." If the scientists are in luck, they may find a summary of such information already prepared; these summaries are often termed "species profiles."

A species profile is a short description of a particular animal or plant species. Such a profile generally provides a biologist with information on the classification of the species, a description of closely related groups of organisms, a summary of the physical and biological traits of the species, and additional information on habits and behaviors of particular interest.

The species profiles of the beaver, the eastern cottontail rabbit, and the gray catbird that follow are presented as they are contained in the reference files of Ecomunk. An Ecomunk keeps such information handy for use in preparing for ecological investigations; the species profiles contain information that is often useful when dealing with individuals of these species. I must admit that I prepared the chipmunk profile myself, using a style similar to that used by the Ecological Society of Chipmunks in preparing their file notes for their Ecomunks.

One note on scientific names. Biologists have the option of referring to an organism by its common name or by its scientific (taxonomic) name. So for example, a house pet could be referred to as a dog or as *Canis familiaris*. The second name, the taxonomic name, is called a Latin binomial (a two-word scientific name phrased in Latin or sometimes in Greek). The first word in the Latin binomial is the genus; it is always capitalized and italicized (or underlined if you are using a typewriter). The second word is the species; it is always lower cased and italicized.

By using such standard scientific names, biologists are able to be precise about what animal or plant they are discussing and in this way avoid confusion that comes from common names. For example, I once had a pet snake that I raised from an egg. He was named Cain and was what Californians commonly call a gopher snake. In Texas, the same species is commonly called a bull snake. When I use the scientific name *Pituophis melanoleucus* when I talk about Cain, all biologists can understand what kind of snake I am talking about.

Species Profile: Eastern Chipmunk

The scientific name of the eastern chipmunk is *Tamias striatus*. The chipmunks, of which there are several North American species, are related to the tree squirrels, ground squirrels, prairie dogs, marmots, and woodchucks (all of these are in the scientific family

Sciuridae). The eastern chipmunk is a small mammal, with a body length of about five to six inches and a bushy tail about three to four inches long. Its fur is brownish red, with black and white stripes over the eyes and across its sides.

Chipmunks build burrows underground, often in rocky areas where many cracks and holes already exist. They eat a wide variety of seeds and nuts and store extra food in chambers of their burrows. In the wintertime, they generally stay in their burrows and conserve energy by lowering their metabolic rate (the amount of energy they use).

Chipmunks are inquisitive little mammals, although they are relatively secretive and shy. They manage to live quite well around the homes and yards of humans and sometimes become bold enough to approach humans for food. They are, however, wild creatures and can bite if humans try to treat them like tame house pets.

Species Profile: Beaver

The scientific name for the beaver is *Castor canadensis*. It is the largest North American rodent, with a body length of twenty-five to thirty inches and a flat, scaly tail about nine to ten inches long. Beavers build stick and mud dams across small streams to form shallow ponds. Their houses, or beaver lodges, are conical structures of sticks and mud built out in the water of their ponds, where they are protected from predators.

The tree-cutting activities of a beaver are central to its life-style. First, like all rodents, its front teeth (incisors) never stop growing, and a beaver must do plenty of gnawing on tree trunks and branches to keep its teeth worn down (sort of like filing down your fingernails). They love to eat the bark of aspens, a tree commonly found in wet areas, and they also eat grass, ferns, and water plants.

The beaver has always been a symbol of hard work; humans use the phrase "busy as a beaver" to describe a hard-working person. Because they love to build dams, they can change the ecology of the area where they live, and in this way they can affect the lives of other animals. Also, they tend to be pretty hard-headed about their beaver-dam projects and don't like to get advice from other animals. So if you must deal with a beaver, you have to praise his engineering skills and make your suggestions about changes in a very polite way.

Species Profile: Eastern Cottontail

The eastern cottontail, the rabbit species most commonly seen in grassy or brushy areas in eastern and central North America, has the scientific name *Sylvilagus floridans*. It belongs to the larger group of mammals termed lagomorphs—the rabbits, hares, and pikas. All lagomorphs have a distinctive arrangement of front teeth (incisors). The incisors of lagomorphs are double, with a second small tooth growing behind the large front incisor.

Eastern cottontails have done very well in the open areas (fields and brush) around human farms. They are shy creatures, generally leaving their burrows in the morning and evening to feed. Even while they are eating leaves of grass or clover (or sometimes, the lettuce in a human's garden), they are constantly listening for strange sounds with those big rabbit ears.

Because the eastern cottontail is a shy, somewhat nervous creature, you must deal with it very calmly and gently. Never get pushy or loud; this will just make it more nervous and may cause it to dive back into its burrow. If you can manage to get a cottontail to sit still and talk, it can tell you a lot of things about the local environment.

Species Profile: Gray Catbird

The scientific name of the gray catbird is *Dumatella carolinensis*. Its close relatives are the mockingbirds and thrashers (family Mimidae). All of these birds are, as the family name implies, good mimics; they can easily repeat sounds that they hear and probably even invent new sounds from their own imaginations.

The catbird has a slate gray color, with a black patch on the top of its head. It is a medium-size, very active bird, often found flying around the edges of woodlands and fields in search of insects and fruit. Catbirds move south for the winter and come back north in the spring when temperatures get warmer.

Although catbirds are very curious, and seem to be in on all the local gossip, they are not very assertive and need to be coaxed into conversation. They are cautious around strange animals and do better when they are talking to someone familiar to them.